First published in Great Britain in 2001 by Brimax
an imprint of Octopus Publishing Group Ltd
2-4 Heron Quays, London E14 4JP
© Octopus Publishing Group Ltd

ISBN 1 8585 4828 4
Printed in China

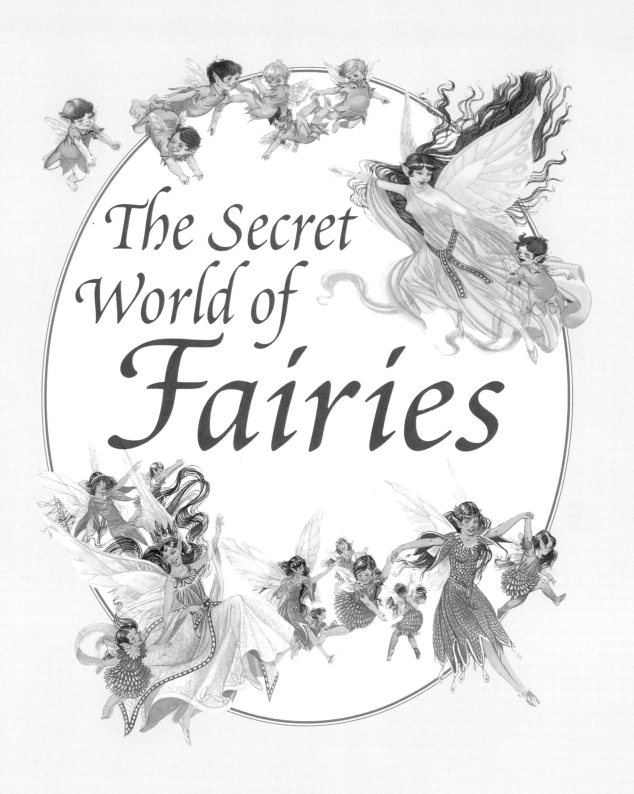

The Secret World of Fairies

BRIMAX

Introduction

When the most beautiful flowers are blooming,
the fairies are in charge of making sure they are
looked after. They fly around the flowers, telling
them how pretty they are and that one day
they too will be fairies.
When the petals fall and thistledown grows
in their place, the fairies tickle and tug the fluffy
down until it lets go and floats up into the sky.
This is how fairies are born.
Have you ever wondered how fairies
get such beautiful wings?
Then read the stories and rhymes inside to find
out about the Snowy, Sunny, Rainy
and Rainbow Fairies…

Contents

Where do fairies come from?

You really want to know.

And are they very tiny,

Or do they sometimes grow?

There are many kinds of fairies,

And most you'll never see.

They hide in secret places,

Like a plant or nest or tree.

In The Secret World of Fairies,
You will have a special treat.
Because some very special fairies,
Are here for you to meet.

Rainbow and Sunny Fairies,
Have gathered on the ground.
With Rainy and Snowy Fairies,
They play and fly around.

Snowy Day Fairies

ONE COLD WINTER DAY it started to snow. The snowflakes on this finger-tingling day were extra large, because this was the day they were bringing down the new Snowy Day fairies.

In the middle of each snowflake was a tiny baby fairy.

The snowflakes *drifted* gently to the ground where the older fairies were waiting for them, radiant and shining in the pale winter sun.

The baby fairies stood up slowly and carefully, wobbling slightly on their chubby baby legs, blinking in the winter brightness as they shook out their little brown wings.

Queen Snowdrop stepped forward to welcome the new fairies.

Her gown was of the finest dazzling white silk with frost crystals sparkling all over it.

The baby fairies looked at her silvery wings in wonder, and then looked at their own small brown ones.

They all felt very glum indeed!

All the older fairies gathered around excitedly as the queen held up her wand. Now was the time for a little fun!

"Babies, you must roll in the snow."

The babies were timid at first, and sat uncertainly in the cold wet snow, until the older fairies shouted out encouragement.

"Roll, roll!"

They laughed as the babies rolled sideways and backwards. Some even went head over heels!

When at last they stood up and shook the loose flakes from their wings all the babies were laughing happily.

Gone were the brown wings and in their place were wings of gleaming white, with sparkles of frost all over them.

But all of that rolling around had left the babies feeling very cold, and they shivered so much that their beautiful wings tinkled as they shook.

"Come along all of you," said Queen Snowdrop, "we must take these babies somewhere cosy where they can warm up and sleep until it stops snowing."

"Where are we going?" asked one of the babies through chattering teeth.

"We shall go to the home of the friendly squirrel. He has a lovely, cosy hole in the oak tree. He lets all sorts of people use it when it is cold."

The queen took the hand of the smallest fairy as she started to lead the way.

They all trooped in fairy file behind the queen as she led them into the wood.

When they reached the dark tunnel where the friendly squirrel lived, the light from the fairies' wings lit it up so much that Squirrel had to blink his eyes to see them.

"Come in, come in,

make yourselves comfortable on the bumblies. They won't mind, they are asleep."

The friendly squirrel pointed to lots of fat bumble bees curled up all over the floor. They looked just like big, furry, brown and yellow cushions!

The older fairies knew what to do and showed the babies how to snuggle down in their soft fur.

Then they all went to sleep safe and warm, as cosy as only a fairy on a bumble bee can be.

And that's how Snowy Day Fairies get such beautiful wings.

The Snowy Day Fairies

Drifting down on icicles,
The fairies flapped their wings.
They had a busy day ahead,
Making magic fairy rings.

Their pure-white gowns glittered,
As snow fell all around.
Those busy little fairies,
Hardly made a sound.

Brushing past some snowdrops,

A tinkling sound rang out.

That's the only way we know,

The fairies are about!

All dancing in a circle,

They cast a magic spell,

To make sure all the wildlife

Are safe and warm and well.

Sunny Day Fairies

ONE DAY, NOT VERY LONG AGO, lots and lots of golden fairies gathered together. They all flocked to where the brightest sunbeams shone down onto the ground from the dazzling sunshine above.

They were waiting for the new fairies. Sunny Day Fairies slide down sunbeams when they come down to the ground, and today was the very day they were due to arrive.

The first baby fairies

floated to the

ground, quickly followed

by six others who had also come down the

sunbeam.

    Their wings were still tightly folded

behind their backs, so the golden fairies

called out excitedly,

    "Do your wings, do your wings."

They all loved that bit the best.

Eric Kincaid

One of the new fairies started to *wriggle* her shoulders and as she did her wings gradually *unfurled*, just like a butterfly's wings. At first the baby fairy was thrilled with her new wings, but then she looked very unhappy and she started to cry.

"What is the matter?" asked one of the grown-up fairies, "Don't you like your wings?"

"I do like my wings," said the baby fairy sadly, "but they are not pretty like yours. Why can't I have lovely golden wings like you?"

"Just wait. Wait for the pollen party, and you'll see," said the older fairy kindly.

When the babies were all together Queen Buttercup stepped forward. She was dressed in a yellow, silken gown, which had tiny buttercups sewn into the hem. As she walked she left a trail of fairy dust.

"Now you must come with us," she said, "we will take you to the buttercup meadow and there you will have a surprise."

Eric Kincaid

All the golden fairies fluttered up into the air, holding hands with the new fairies, as some of them couldn't fly very well.

"Now," said Queen Buttercup, "are we all here?" "Yes!" squealed the babies in excitement. "We are! We are!"

And so they flew high into the air and over the countryside until they reached the golden buttercup meadow.

Once they were all there, Queen Buttercup told the older fairies to take the babies to the buttercups. There was much laughter as the brown and grey winged fairies were led to the tall golden flowers.

"Now fairies," said Queen Buttercup, "stand the babies under the flowers." As they were led to the flowers they looked up in wonder at the shining yellow petals of the buttercups above their heads.

The older fairies took hold of the flower stalks and when Queen Buttercup waved her wand the fairies shook the flowers as hard as their slender arms would let them.

The fairies were so happy that they laughed and danced and fluttered all afternoon.

When they were tired they curled up and went to sleep in the empty birds' nests scattered about the hedge, to dream of the fun they would have together on all the sunny days to come.

And that's how Sunny Day Fairies get such **beautiful** wings.

Sunny Day Fairies

The Sunny Day Fairies arrived,
On a sunbeam of glowing gold.
The babies loved the sunshine,
And were glad it wasn't cold.

Standing beneath some buttercups,
One baby shook her head.
She wished her wings were yellow,
Not dull and brown instead.

Then much to her surprise she saw,
As pollen floated down,
The colour of her wings changed -
And were no longer brown!

Then all the golden fairies,
Babies and grown-ups, too,
Followed behind Queen Buttercup.
As into the air she flew.

Rainy Day Fairies

W

HEN THE GARDEN
was dripping wet, just a few days after the
thistledown had drifted up to the sky, out of
the fat grey clouds came

extra large,

shiny,

raindrops.

Clinging on to each raindrop was a new
Rainy Day Fairy. Waiting for the babies
were the older fairies, who had come
down on raindrops last year.

As the new fairies plopped to the ground they
stood up slowly and unfurled their wings.

They didn't unfurl them like other
fairies did, but shook them - just like a dog.

This made all the older fairies
scream as they were sprayed with rainwater.
The baby fairies stood looking at the

beautiful wings of the older

fairies. And then they looked

sadly at their own, which

were brown.

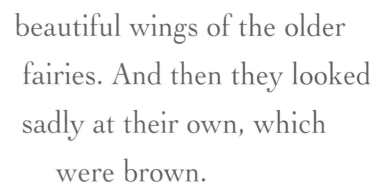

Queen Raindrop

smiled at them and held out her hands.
"Come along little ones, don't be sad,
I'm going to show you how to make your
wings as beautiful as mine, and
it won't take very long. Just do as I say."

Queen Raindrop led them to a large
puddle in the lane by the wood, followed by
all the older fairies who whispered and
giggled in excitement.

When the fairies were gathered round, Queen Raindrop said,

"This is a very special puddle and you must all wash your wings in it. This puddle is a gift from the dragon-flies, who leave all the shades of green and blue in the water for the new fairies.

When you have finished, your wings will look just like ours.

Now off you go babies, and splash as much as you like."

The new babies splashed and laughed, watched by the queen and the older fairies.

Some fat white ducks were watching too, and as you know they love to be out in the rain, especially when the new fairies have arrived.

After a little while the queen said, "Stop now, that should be enough. Now we must get you dry."

That said, she put her hand to her mouth and called softly into the reeds by the stream. In a flash of gleaming blue feathers, a kingfisher arrived and hovered over the fairies.

"The babies must be dried Kingfisher, if you please. Will you do it?"

The kingfisher blinked at the wet babies and flew to a large mushroom.

"You must each of you climb onto the giant mushroom and hold out your wings," said Queen Raindrop.

With the help of the older fairies all of the babies climbed onto the mushroom and shyly held out their wings.

When they were ready the beautiful kingfisher flew over each of them in turn and hovered over them. He flapped his wings so fast that you could barely see them move.

In no time at all the babies' wings were dry, and they were astonished and delighted as they began to change! Sparkling aqua-marines started to shine through the brown and shimmered in the watery sunlight.

The baby fairies flew from the mushroom to join the Queen and the older fairies.

As they were brand new fairies, they were soon very tired, and were taken to their new home under the damp, dripping bushes next to the river, where they slept.

But only for a short while, as when they awoke they had a whole new world to explore...

And that's how Rainy Day Fairies get such **beautiful** wings.

The Rainy Day Fairies

The Rainy Day Fairies arrived,
On raindrops they fell from the sky.
Down to the ground they tumbled,
As they hadn't yet learned to fly.

Splashing around in puddles,
The babies were having fun.
Playing in the sparkling water,
Their tiny wings glowed in the sun.

When it was time to learn to fly,
The babies had so much trouble.
They thought it would be easier,
If they all drifted round in a bubble!

But the older fairies just laughed,
And showed them what to do.
And soon those baby fairies,
Were flapping their tiny wings, too.

Brushing past some snowdrops,
A tinkling sound rang out.
That's the only way we know,
The fairies are about!

Rainbow Fairies

ONE DAY IN THE COUNTRYSIDE when the thunder and lightning had stopped, a beautiful arch appeared in the blue sky. It was an arch of red, orange, yellow, green, blue, indigo and violet.

It was called a **rainbow**. This was the time when the Rainbow Fairies arrived.

It was always very exciting when the new Rainbow Fairies arrived, and all the older Rainbow Fairies gathered at the end of the rainbow to greet them.

As soon as the rainbow appeared in the sky, the baby Rainbow Fairies started to *slide* down the arch. Rainbow Fairies didn't come very often, but when they did there were lots and lots of them.

Unlike other types of fairy, the Rainbow Fairies arrived with wings already beautiful, for as they slid down the rainbow it brushed against them, painting them in all its lovely shades.

Eric Kincaid

They bounced onto the grass and their wings *sparkled* as they tried flapping them for the very first time.

But there was one baby fairy who could not flap because one of her delicate little wings was torn.

The older fairies gathered around and tried to comfort her, but the poor little fairy was much too upset!

Queen Rainbow flew over and gently took the fairy by the hand. "Don't cry little one, we'll soon have that wing mended, and then you can fly with the other fairies."

"But how will you mend something so fine?" sobbed the baby fairy.

"We shall take you to a master who spins only the finest silk," replied the queen.

Queen Rainbow led the fairies through the grass to the bush where Old Spinny had his web and workshop.

When they arrived the fairies made a circle around the bush. Then Queen Rainbow went up to the cobweb, and *gently* touched it with her magical wand.

It was just enough to bring out the largest, friendliest spider you have ever seen. The spider crawled onto a large stone and looked up at Queen Rainbow.

"Hello, Old Spinny," she said, stroking his head.

"Would you be so kind as to mend this baby's wing? I think she was too excited and came down the rainbow much too fast."

"Well, well," said Old Spinny. "Turn around and let me see what you have done." He put on a large pair of spectacles to see more clearly...

"Yes, I see the trouble, that little tear won't take long to fix."

And he winked at the baby, who smiled back shyly.

Old Spinny carefully tucked a thread of finest gossamer into the torn wing. Then he started to turn around as the silk came out of the cobweb sac at the back of his body.

He turned delicately one way, and then another, until the tear was completely mended.

All this time the fairies had stood watching in *wonder* as the baby fairy's wing was made as good as new. Then the fairies cheered loudly as the baby flew up and down in delight.

Old Spinny gave what was left of his fine thread to the birds for their nests, and the fairies said goodbye to the kind and friendly spider.

Darkness was starting to fall over the fairy dell, and normally this is the time the baby fairies would go to bed. But not tonight, for a rainbow day is a special day, and tonight was just right for a party.

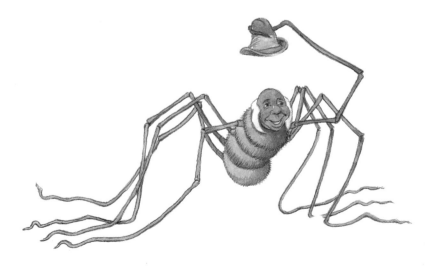

The Rainbow Fairies

Red, Orange, yellow, green,

Blue, indigo and violet, too.

A rainbow appeared in the sky,

Which grew and grew and grew!

Lots of fairy babies,

Slid down the rainbow arch,

One behind the other,

They all began to march.

One baby's wing was torn,

Which made her very sad.

How would she ever learn to fly,

With the tattered wing she had?

Old Spinny had the answer,

And a silken thread he made.

The other fairies watched him,

As the baby's wing he saved.

Where do fairies go to,

When stars come out at night?

They gather all together,

And dance in the moonlight.

Their pretty wings flutter,

As they skip between the flowers.

Round and round the fairies go,

Singing for hours and hours.

Perhaps you've even heard them,
Just before you go to bed.
Perhaps you've even seen them,
Flying just above your head.

But always, always remember,
That fairies are sometimes there.
And if you ever see one,
Please try not to stare.